PirateS AHoy!

Created by small world creations ltd

igloo

Kate and Jessica were having a tea party. Suddenly Sam leaped out from behind the curtain dressed like a pirate.

"Go away!" shouted Kate.

"Mum!" yelled Jessica.

"You're my prisoners!" hissed Pirate Sam.

Kate and Jessica didn't want to be prisoners.

"We'll be pirates too," they told Sam.

"And we'll be braver and fiercer than you!"

Pirate Sam's boat was an upside-down table.
Pirate Kate and Pirate Jessica used their dolly's crib.

"Pretend we're in the middle of the sea and my boat's the fastest!" yelled Pirate Sam.

Pirate Kate began to rock the crib.

"There's a storm," she cried. "The waves are too high - help, we're sinking!"

The children rocked from side to side until they spilled out onto the carpet.

"It's lucky there's a beach nearby," said Pirate Sam, scrambling onto the rug.

"This island's too small," said Pirate Kate.

"There's more room outside," suggested Pirate Sam.

So they went outside and pretended that the garden was their secret island.

"These are my coconuts," said Pirate Sam, gathering up all the balls. He threw one at Pirate Jessica. "I'm still the bravest, fiercest pirate!" he yelled.

"Oh no you're not!" shouted Pirate Kate, throwing a ball back at him.

"Missed!" said Sam, ducking.

"It's getting dark," said Pirate Jessica. "Let's go indoors and build a shelter for the night." Inside, Jessica put up the umbrella. They collected boxes and toys and logs and built a den. It was cosy under the umbrella, and they pretended that there was a storm outside.

Sam made howling noises like the wind, and Kate made kaboom noises like thunder.

"Lucky we've got the torch," whispered Pirate Jessica.

"Sssh, there's wild animals outside," said Pirate Kate, pointing at the dog.

"He's eating our coconuts," giggled Pirate Sam.

"It's morning now," said Pirate Jessica, standing up and stretching.

"Look - we're on a treasure island," said Pirate Kate and she quickly found a piece of chalk and drew a treasure map. They ran around, crawling and climbing over pretend plants and rocks, following the pretend map.

"I've found the treasure!"
cried Pirate Kate running out with a box of cookies.

"Hurray" shouted Pirate Sam, racing over for his share of the tasty treat.

"This island is full of treasure,"
said Pirate Jessica.

They ate their cookies inside. Mum had put the vacuum cleaner in the middle of the floor.

"Help! I'm being cuddled by a big blue snake!" shouted Pirate Sam, wrapping the hose around his body

"Quick, run for the boats," cried Pirate Kate, "and don't forget the treasure!"

The pirates jumped into the dolly's crib and rowed away from the snake using Mum's wooden spoons as oars.

Then they jumped into Pirate Sam's upside-down table and played 'walk the plank' using a rug as the plank and a scarf to blindfold the victim. "I can't swim," said Pirate Kate, pretending to be scared.

"Don't worry - the water isn't very deep," giggled Pirate Jessica.

"We need a ghost ship," said Pirate Kate.
"Every good adventure story should have a ghost ship."
They pretended the cupboard was a ghostly galleon.

"Let's explore it,"
suggested Pirate Sam,
clutching the torch.

The cupboard was full of hangers and piles of old clothes. It made a wonderful ghost ship.

"What was that?" whispered Pirate Jessica.

"What?"
said Pirate Kate

"This!" cried Pirate Sam. He threw a white blanket over his head and chased the girls out of the cupboard. "I'm a ghost," he yelled. "Get off my ship!"

"Help!" squealed Pirate Kate. "Back to the boat!"

Mum was vacuuming the carpet and had moved the upside-down table into the garden.

"Let's pretend the waves have carried away our boat and we have to search for it on the high seas," suggested Pirate Jessica.

They ran outside.

"This is my boat and I'm the captain," said Pirate Kate.
"It was my boat first," said Pirate Sam. "And this is my game."

"Can't we share the ship and the game?" said Pirate Jessica.

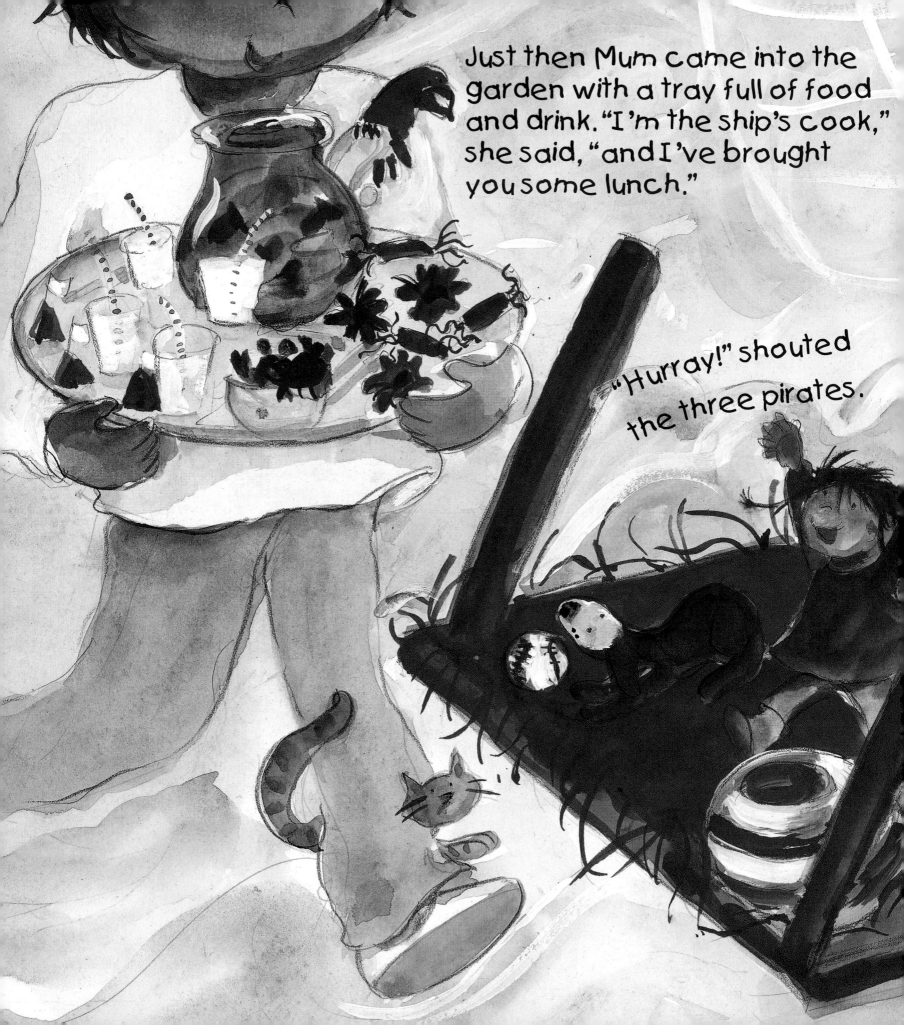

Just then Mum came into the garden with a tray full of food and drink. "I'm the ship's cook," she said, "and I've brought you some lunch."

"Hurray!" shouted the three pirates.

"Let's pretend the squash is rum punch," suggested Pirate Kate.

"Is that octopus spread in those sandwiches?"
giggled Pirate Sam.

"I like tea-parties best," said Jessica.